Dedicated to F. & R., without whom I might never have set sail

Captain Lackbuck

THE PERFECT PIRATE

Flibber T. Gibbet

ISBN-13: 9781726472630
ISBN-10: 1726472639

The pirate LaPlank was so strict on his ship
that he never forgave a mistake or a slip.
He expected perfection — no ifs, ands, or buts.
When it came to mistakes even one made him nuts.

The captain had kind of high standards for crew —
if he could be perfect then they could be too.
All his crew had to do was to do as he did
since a single mistake meant him blowing his lid.

At the sight of his ship other pirates would flip
and decide it was wise to steer clear of his grip.
From Big Booty Bay the whole way to Cave Cove,
he'd clear out the waters wherever he'd rove.

LAKE BUCCANEER

BIG BOOTY
BAY

He would soak any folk he caught beaching, asleep,
and light up his cannons at night like a creep.
And so he'd been chosen, some say out of fear,
as Lake Buccaneer's 'Buccaneer of the Year'.

3

CAVE COVE

With his ship now equipped he climbed up on a box
that he liked to stand up on to heighten his talks.
He called for the crew. They were new to his ship
so he laid down the law before launching the trip.

"For treasure we sail," said LaPlank with a grin,
"but let me say somethin' before we begin.
I'm not much for mistakes, and I mean that sincerely.
Any pirate who makes one will pay for it dearly."

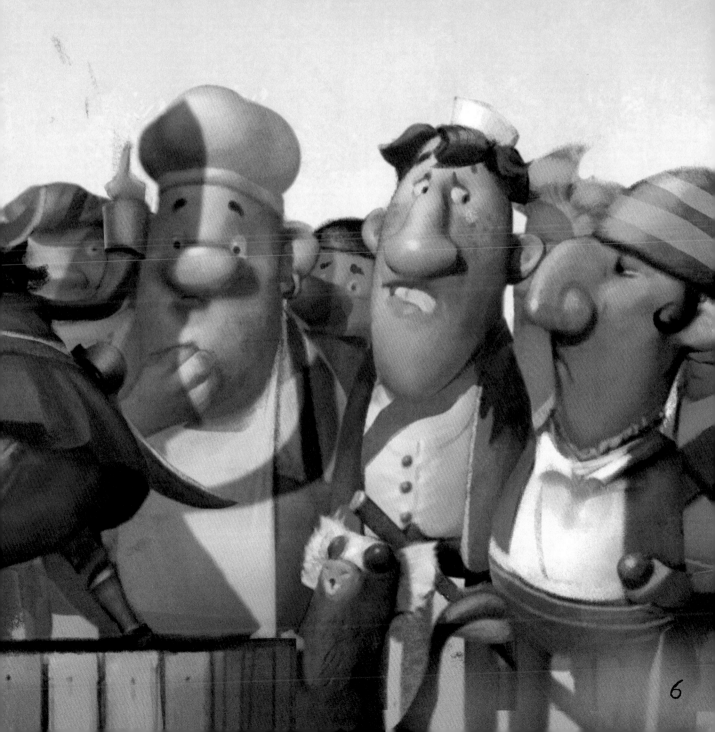

He grabbed a long board from the deck with a yank
and fixed it in place on his ship as a plank.
His pirates each took a quick step to the rear
since planks can be rather unsafe to be near.

"So yer eager to leave!" said LaPlank to his crew.
"But this ship doesn't move till inspection is through.
Now return to yer spots for ya've nothing to fear —
except for mistakes, to be painfully clear."

They did as he ordered. Then he took a minute
to look in a chest and review what was in it.
He gave a great grunt before closing the chest
and commencing inspection with plenty of zest.

He checked on the masts. Then he checked on the sails.
But that was not all — he got down to details.
He checked every knot. Then he checked every line
by tugging and pulling but found they were fine.

He checked every cannon. He checked every ball.
He checked every pistol. But that was not all.
He checked every barrel. He checked every sack.
He checked every flag to make sure it was black.

The crew watched him at work. Would he spot some mistake?
The suspense grew more tense than lake pirates could take.
They bit at their fingers. They sucked on their thumbs.
They screamed for no reason. They called for their mums!

But Captain LaPlank went on checking and checking
without much concern for whose nerves he was wrecking
until at long last there was nothing unchecked
and he had to admit it — why, things were correct!

He called for his pirates. He told them, "Well done.
I could find no mistakes 'coz in fact there were none."
His crew then let loose with much hooting and squealing
and even some tears at the cheer they were feeling.

"Ahoy!" said LaPlank. "That ole west wind is blowin'
so don't ya suppose it's now time to get goin'?"
"Make sail!" he commanded. He brandished his sword
and ran back and forth while his pirates rip roared.

They sprang to the anchor and cranked it up fast
and set every sail into place on its mast
as the piper performed for the pirates at work
while twirling and dancing and acting berserk.

The sails filled with wind. The main mast made a creak
and their ship zipped away from that bay like a streak
while his crew at their posts did their duties so well
that their captain felt happy, though no one must tell.

The weather was splendid. They sailed in the sun.
And there weren't any blunders — except for the one.

LaPlank was astounded. He found it concerning.
His sniffer could whiff it — their burgers were burning!
He turned to the cook and the look that he gave him
soon made it clear that now nothing could save him.

"Mistake!" cried the captain. He threw down his hat and the trampling he gave it soon made that hat flat. The cook looked around. He'd decided to hide but barrels are narrow while pirates are wide.

"To the plank!" said the captain. He captured the cook
and booted his bottom each step that he took.
They stood at the plank. Would the cook be corrected?
The captain glanced down at the chest he'd inspected.

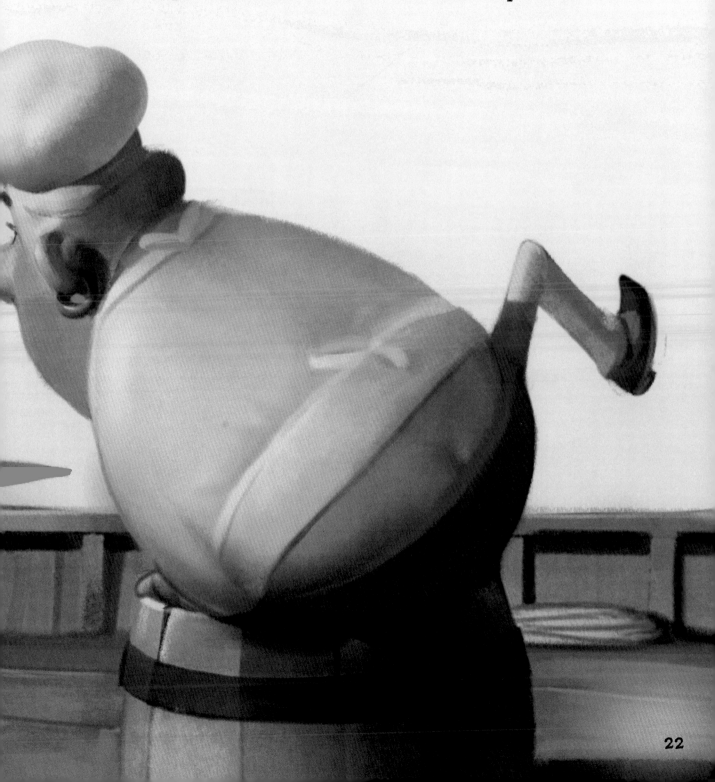

He lifted the lid and inside there were vests,
which every fine captain provides for their guests.
He took the cook's coat and the hat from his head
and then lent him a vest to go floating instead.

Kerplunk, he was dunked! And then left there to bob,
which is no way to go your first day on the job.
The crew was afraid. They all shivered and shook
and shedded some tears at the canning of cook.

"Enough of mistakes!" called the captain to crew,
who returned to their duties as crewmen will do.

The weather stayed splendid. They sailed in the sun.
And there were no more blunders — except for the one.

LaPlank was astounded. He frowned at the deck.
It should've been spotless but there was a speck!
The swabbie's top job was to keep the ship clean,
and specks on his deck made the captain get mean.

"Mistake!" cried the captain. The swabbie said "Sorry"
but his boss wasn't fond of his I'm-sorry-story.
From his chest he selected a vest from on top,
which he handed the swabbie instead of his mop.

Kerplunk, he was dunked! Then the ship sailed away and he shrank to a speck in the rear-view display. "Enough of mistakes!" called the captain to crew, who returned to their duties as crewmen will do.

The weather stayed splendid. They sailed in the sun.
And there were no more blunders — except for the one.

LaPlank was astounded. To starboard, he'd said,
so why was this ship of his porting instead?
He yelled for his helmsman, whose duty was steering
and who wore a big horn in each ear for his hearing.

"Mistake!" cried the captain. His helmsman said "Sonny?",
which his boss did not hold on the whole to be funny.
He unhorned his helmsman like that in a flash
and then lent him a vest to help soften the splash.

Kerplunk, he was dunked! And then left there to simmer
for the helmsman was not a strong long-distance swimmer.
"Enough of mistakes!" called the captain to crew,
who returned to their duties as crewmen will do.

But the blunders kept coming. Their numbers grew bigger.
He was giving out vests to the crew with some vigor.
Kerplunk, they were dunked! Some may find this surprising
but it looked like that lake might have actually been rising.

The pirates all tried to not anger LaPlank
but their minor mistakes made the captain a crank.
His crew he'd all booted, excluding their piper,
who had grown so scared he was wearing a diaper.

But his piping was perfect. He'd nothing to dread —
except that their captain kept losing his head.
The captain looked frantic. He'd far too much work
after booting his crew like some kind of a jerk.

He did all the cooking, the cleaning, and steering
in a fearsome display of extreme buccaneering.
His new problem was jobs. He had rather too many.
But then where was the fun? He was not having any.

While the captain was acting as crew for his ship,
his piper's fine fingers just happened to slip.
The piper fell silent while over the boat
there rang out the sound of a slightly wrong note.

"Mistake!" cried the captain, unlatching that chest
before reaching inside to retrieve him his vest.
When his fingers found nothing inside except air,
all the captain could do was to bend down and stare.

His stomach did cartwheels. His heart hopped a beat
and his shoulders dipped so low they touched both his feet.
The poor piper kept quiet while the tension now mounted.
That chest was unvested 'coz their captain miscounted!

He'd blundered their numbers like some kind of dummy,
which must have been why all his feelings were crummy.
A disaster had happened on Buccaneer Lake —
the mad captain himself had just made a mistake!

In the midst of his madness the captain stopped short
for he'd thought up some notion that brought up a snort.
All the bunglers before were now very much wetter
for their captain had called for his crew to do better.

But he hadn't himself, which soon set him to thinking —
what happens to captains when they do the stinking?
"What rot!" LaPlank thought. "A ship captain misacting?
It was crew who made booboos. A captain's exacting!"

His confusion now grew. "Are ya captain or chump?"
he asked of himself as he scratched at his stump.
So he thought without stopping. Smoke shot out each ear
till the facts of that matter at last became clear.

It had nothing to do with ship captains and crews —
perfection's not something that pirates can choose.
They'd bungled their business but those are the breaks —
mistakes are just something that everyone makes!

"Uh oh. ." said LaPlank. He looked over his ship,
which had shedded more pirates the longer their trip.
LaPlank looked around at those empty old decks
and considered perfection's less pleasant effects.

"Reverse course!" LaPlank ordered. He snapped a salute and whipped his ship round to shoot back up their route. He rescued his crew. Then he cooked them some cocoa and promised mistakes wouldn't make him go loco.

And that oath was no joke. The 'mad captain' had changed from that prickly old stickler who'd grow so deranged. Deck specks and burned burgers still happened sometimes but mistakes of all kinds did not rate as great crimes.

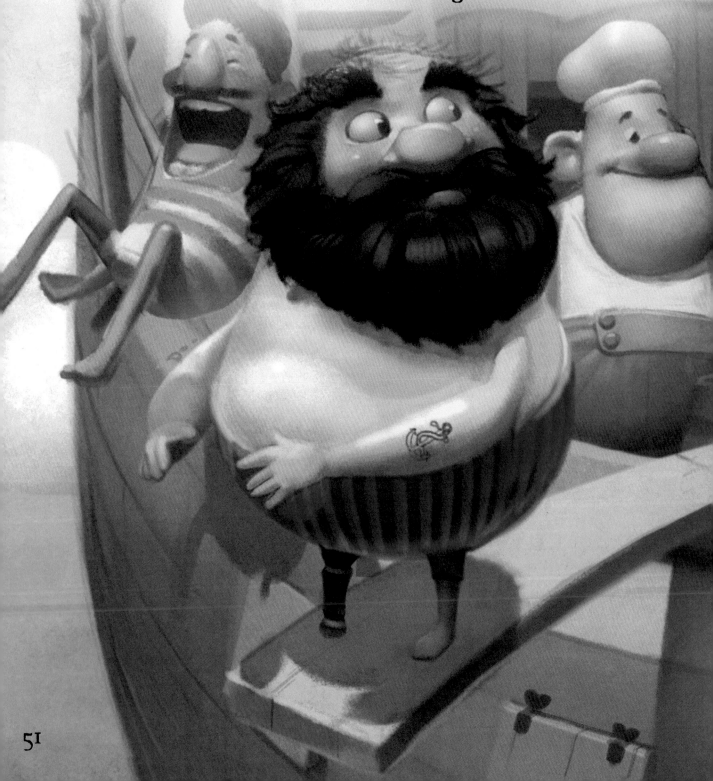

He'd shrug and remind them that those are the breaks —
"Mistakes are just something that everyone makes!"
And that nasty old plank? It was now much adored
for it found a new use. . as the high-diving board.

AUTHOR'S NOTE

Ahoy!

To watch the free story video or to claim your free colouring book, please visit

www.misterflibber.com/buried-treasure

Mister Flibber T. Gibbet,
Lake Buccaneer, Fall 2018
p.s. If you enjoyed the book, would you consider leaving the captain a review? It would be much appreciated!

Made in the USA
Lexington, KY
20 March 2019